Pride Comes Before the Fall

BRAVE BOOKS

Freedom Island

DOM-A-TRON

Doomsdome

THE OLD ISLANDS

Burrycanter

UTOPIA

WIGGAMORE WOOD

Rushington

Hive Have

SUMA SAVANNA

Furenzy park

Toke-A-Toxe

Wonder Well

Capital

Mushroom Village

Deserted Desert

Mt. Avalerif

RAKA RAIN FOREST

Sky Tree

Snapfast Meadow

CAR-A-LAGO COAST

Starlotte City

Gray Landing

Home of the Brave

Welcome to Freedom Island, Home of the Brave, where good battles evil and truth prevails. Join Valor and Kevin as they learn about humility and the dangers of pride when they compete in the Great Raka Rapids Race. Complete the BRAVE Challenge at the end of the book to learn more!

Watch this video for an introduction to the story and BRAVE Universe!

Saga Three: Tubular

Book 4

Pride Comes Before the Fall

Saga Three: Tubular—Book 4

Pride Comes Before the Fall

Copyright © 2023 by BRAVE BOOKS
All Rights Reserved

Book Illustrations © 2023 by Steve Crespo
Map Illustration © 2021 by Ali Elzeiny

Published by BRAVE BOOKS
www.BRAVEbooks.com

ISBN: 978-1-955550-39-0 (paperback)

First edition published in the USA in 2023 by BRAVE BOOKS

Printed in Canada

Pride Comes Before the Fall

Kirk Cameron and BRAVE BOOKS

Art by Steve Crespo

BRAVE BOOKS

Valor's grin was wider than a mile. Today, he would compete in the Great Raka Rapids Race, and he was confident that he was going to win.

Valor and his friends gathered at Mushroom Falls for the race every summer. Only, this year, things were not going quite as he had expected.

"Hey Rebel!" Asher called to the cheetah.

"Do you want to be my partner?"

Rebel grinned. "For sure!"

Near the starting line, Bongo gave Eva a high-paw.
"Dude, we're so going to win this thing."

Valor couldn't believe it. If Asher was with Rebel and
Bongo was with Eva, that left Valor without a partner.
He was smart and strong! Why didn't they choose him?

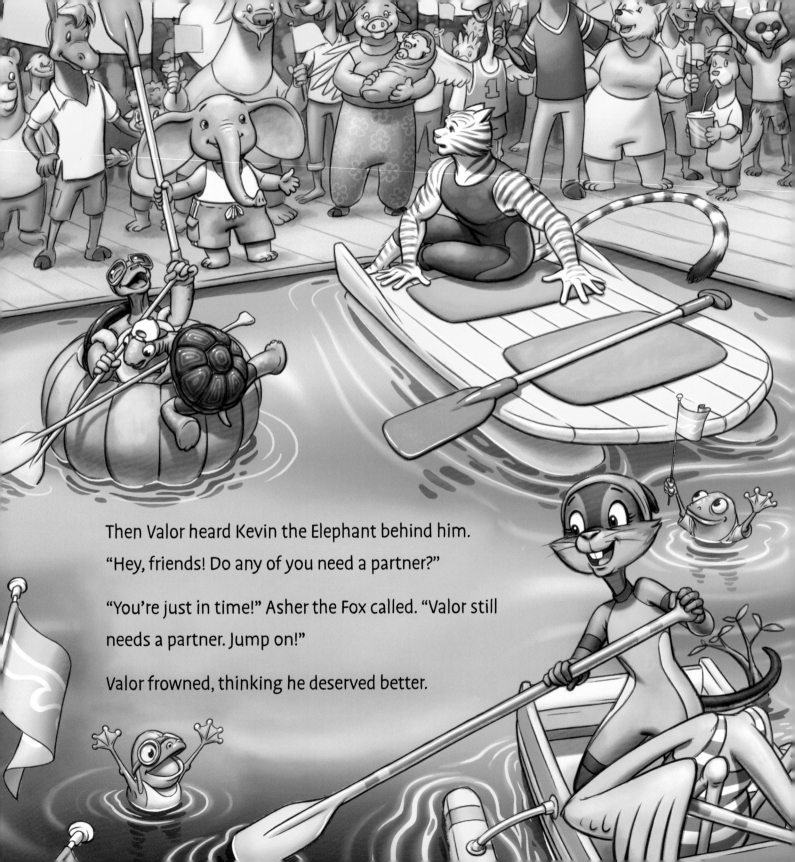

Then Valor heard Kevin the Elephant behind him.
"Hey, friends! Do any of you need a partner?"

"You're just in time!" Asher the Fox called. "Valor still
needs a partner. Jump on!"

Valor frowned, thinking he deserved better.

Kevin was nice but ... he was a lot better at singing than paddling. Before Valor could say anything, Kevin hopped aboard.

The cannon blasted, and the rafts took off!

Asher and Rebel zoomed forward on their high tech raft, while Bongo and Eva pushed ahead with powerful strokes. Everyone was doing great! Well, almost everyone.

"Oh, sorry." Kevin winced. "I've never paddled a raft before. Is this right?"

Valor rolled his eyes. *Why do I get the partner who has no idea what he's doing,* Valor thought to himself. *I am the best athlete here.*

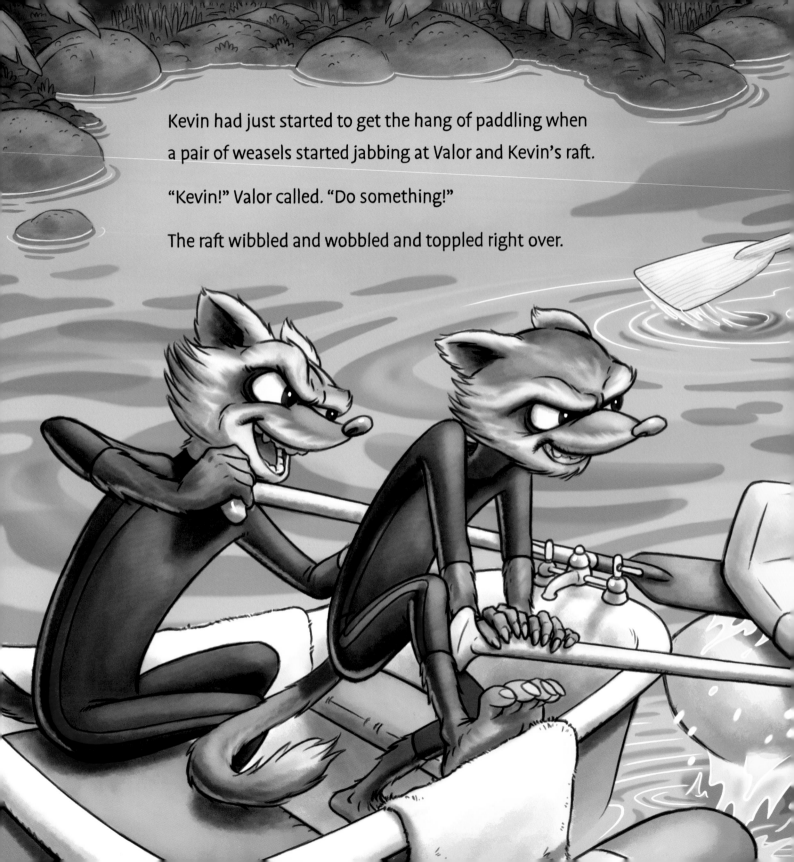

Kevin had just started to get the hang of paddling when a pair of weasels started jabbing at Valor and Kevin's raft.

"Kevin!" Valor called. "Do something!"

The raft wibbled and wobbled and toppled right over.

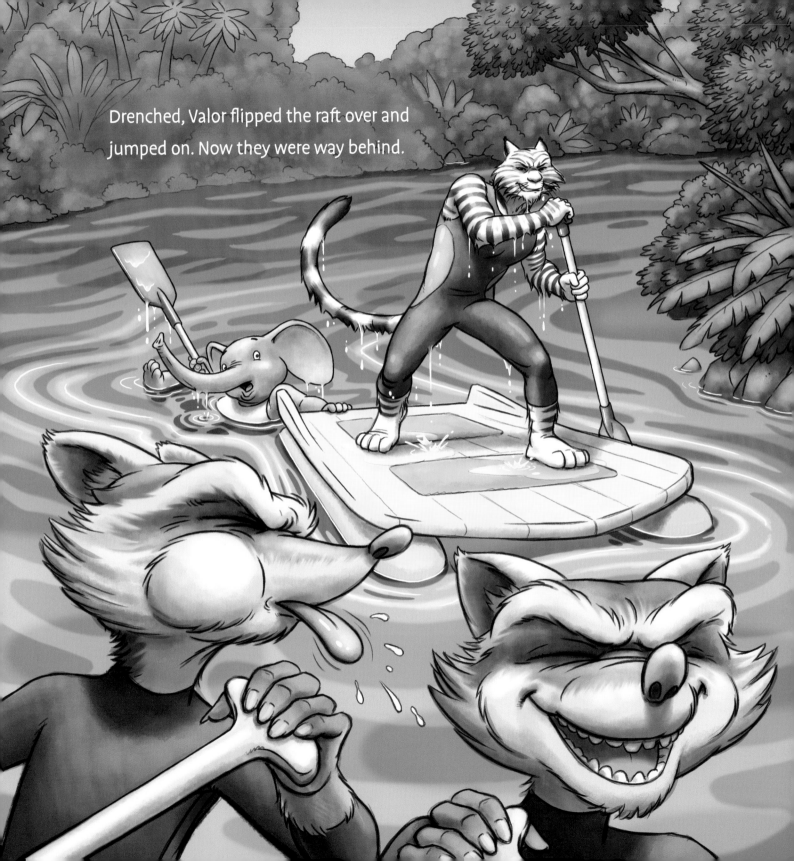

Drenched, Valor flipped the raft over and jumped on. Now they were way behind.

"I can't believe this, Kevin!" Valor slammed his oar down. "Why do you have to mess everything up?"

Kevin turned away.

CRACK!

"Oh no!" What had he done? Valor looked at his oar. He had broken it when he slammed it down in anger.

"Wait." Kevin's ear flicked.

"Do you hear that?"

Valor heard a deep rumbling downstream.
They had reached the Great Raka Falls!

"Kevin! Kevin! I need your oar right away!"
Valor grabbed Kevin's oar. But he was too late.

They spun and spun and ...

At the bottom of the waterfall, Valor started pulling their raft from the rainforest. He was beginning to realize that their problems weren't all Kevin's fault.

If Valor hadn't broken his oar, they would have rafted down the waterfall successfully.

"Look what I found, Valor!" Kevin held out a large branch. "I could use this branch to paddle, then you could have my oar. Maybe we can still win the race!"

Valor smiled. "Thanks for offering your oar, but it's my fault we only have one. The tree branch won't be as easy to use, so you keep the paddle, and I'll take the branch."

Kevin grinned, "Let's do this!"

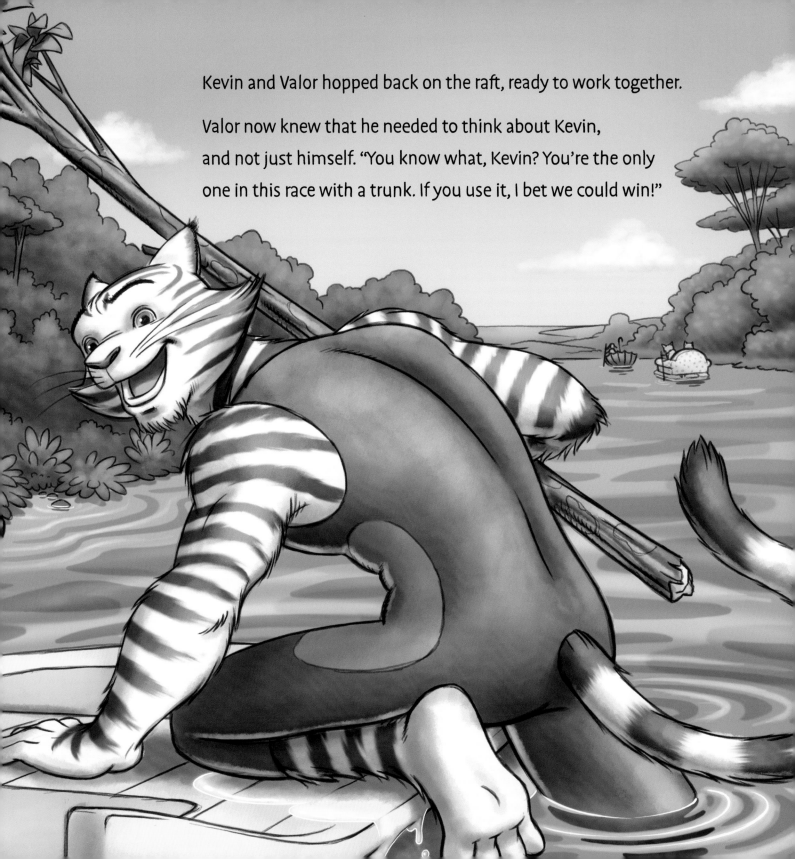

Kevin and Valor hopped back on the raft, ready to work together.

Valor now knew that he needed to think about Kevin, and not just himself. "You know what, Kevin? You're the only one in this race with a trunk. If you use it, I bet we could win!"

Soon, they were flying down the river, passing other teams left and right.

"You're doing great!" Valor called out over the sound of water blasting from Kevin's trunk.

"We've got this, Kevin!" shouted
Valor. "I can see the finish line!"

The crowd cheered as Kevin and Valor crossed the finish line ... in second place.

Kevin sighed, "Sorry we didn't get first, Valor."

Valor smiled. "Kevin, we would have come in last if it weren't for you. Please forgive me for only thinking about myself. And thank you for sticking with me, even when I wasn't a great friend."

"Absolutely, I forgive you." Kevin said. "That's what friends do."

THE TWIGSDALE TIMES

Top Stories from the Sky Tree Canopy

DYNAMIC DUO UNLOCKS NEW RACING TECHNIQUE TO CLAIM SECOND PLACE

ANYONE FIND A LOST BATHTUB?

Items can go missing from time to time: wallets, toys, even socks. But when we heard there was a "missing bathtub," we did a double-take. Local resident says that the new bathtub she ordered had disappeared from her front porch. "I'm more impressed than angry." Pelly the pelican said. "I guess I'll have to get a new bird bath." There are no leads at this time, but eye witnesses say they saw a couple of weasels sneaking around Pelly's Place over the weekend.

COMIC CORNER

> Boy, this place sure is *desserted!*

> Uhh, don't you mean *deserted?*

> No.

BRAVE CADETS,

Valor and Kevin have come in a close 2nd in The Great Raka Rapids Race. But the next race might be tricky as well. Complete the two missions below to help Valor and Kevin!

- Help Valor and Kevin in the BRAVE Challenge, and celebrate your victory with an epic reward.

- Can you find the umbrella raft with Seymour Clues and Mr. Mouse on it 6 times in the story?

Valor and Kevin are counting on you! Are you ready to be BRAVE?

KEVIN: THE NATURAL RAFTER

"I'm not a natural!" Kevin the elephant exclaimed. "I really just learned how to paddle during the race." Kevin continued to try and hide his rafting secrets, but we all know deep down there's more than meets the eye. Never underestimate an elephant from Toke-A-Toke.

FREEDOM DAY FLAG FACTS

In the tops where Sky Tree grew, our symbol was made anew, swaying in the wind in a vibrant red, white, and blue. When we see the Freedom Island flag flutter in the wind, thank the skilled hands of Twigsdale. High up in the canopy of Sky Tree, the seamstresses of Twigsdale created the Freedom Island flag to represent our love for Freedom Island.

THE BRAVE CHALLENGE

INTRODUCING...
KIRK CAMERON

Kirk Cameron, is a Christian, producer, actor, television and film icon, loving husband, and father. In addition, Kirk has had a big impact on our society through films like *Fireproof*, *The Homeschool Awakening*, and *Lifemark*. He and his wife, Chelsea, live in California and have six children. Kirk Cameron has joined with BRAVE Books in creating *Pride Comes Before the Fall*, a book on humility and the dangers of pride.

KIRK SUGGESTS:

"Hey families! This is my second book with BRAVE, and I am so excited to share this BRAVE Challenge with you and your family. I hope you enjoy these fun games as you learn about humility."

INTRODUCTION

The Great Raka Rapids Race is about to begin! Your mission for this BRAVE Challenge is to help Valor and Kevin win the race. To get started, grab a sheet of paper and a pencil.

If your team can earn 10 points by the end of both games, you have won the challenge!

Before starting Game #1, choose a prize for winning. For example ...

- Going to the pool
- Having a tasty treat
- Playing a board game
- Whatever gets your kiddos excited!

GAME #1 - ACTING OUT?

LESSON
Prideful actions and words hurt the people we love.

OBJECTIVE
Valor's prideful attitude is leading to words and actions that are causing problems during the race! BRAVE Cadets, help Valor recognize how his pride is harming those around him.

MATERIALS
Prop list: Plastic cup, jar with lid, and a piece of paper/pencil.

INSTRUCTIONS

Setup:

1. Choose one cadet for the first round.

2. A parent will whisper to the cadet what he or she will say and act out.

3. The other cadets are the audience, and will guess if the cadet is showing pride or humility after the cadet has finished acting it out.

4. After each round, choose a different cadet. There are 6 rounds.

Round 1: The cadet will yell out, "Why wasn't I picked for your team?!" Then the cadet will cross their arms and say, "I'm way better than he is."

Round 2: The cadet will say, "You just took the last piece of pizza," and then will say, "That's alright you can have it."

Round 3: (Props: paper/pencil) The cadet will use a volunteer. The volunteer will pretend to be a teacher and hold a piece of paper that has 2 + 2 = ? written on it. They will ask the cadet if they can solve the math problem. The cadet will say, "I already know how to solve it, so don't ask me."

Round 4: (Has a prop: jar) The cadet will use a volunteer. The cadet will pretend to be struggling with opening a jar. The volunteer will ask if they want help opening the jar. The cadet will then yell, "I don't need any help!"

Round 5: (Has props: paper/pencil) The cadet will use a volunteer. The cadet will sit down with a piece of paper and pen in front of him and say, "I'm not sure what the answer is to this math problem." The volunteer will then help the cadet with the math problem. The cadet will then respond with, "Thank you for the help."

Round 6: (Has a prop: empty cup) Place the cup near the edge of a table. The cadet will walk by the table and will pretend to accidentally knock over the cup. Then the cadet will say, "It wasn't my fault. Someone else put it too close to the edge."

ANSWER KEY

Round 1 = pride   Round 4 = pride
Round 2 = humility   Round 5 = humility
Round 3 = pride   Round 6 = pride

TALK ABOUT IT

1. What do you think pride means?

KIRK SUGGESTS:

"Pride is focusing on yourself rather than putting others first. For example, always having to be first, talking about yourself a lot, not being thankful, complaining, or even blaming others."

2. In the game you had to act out different responses. Were the prideful responses easy to recognize? Why?

3. Do you think it's always clear when we are being prideful? Why?

"Do nothing from selfish ambition or conceit, but in humility count others more significant than yourselves. Let each of you look not only to his own interests, but also to the interests of others."

Philippians 2:3-4 (ESV)

4. Give 2 to 3 examples from the story of when Valor was acting prideful. How would Valor have responded differently if he was humble?

ONE CHILD MODIFICATION

Have the parents read the statements and act them out for the cadet to guess.

SCORING

If the cadets in the audience guess the response correctly, they receive 1 point. If a cadet says what type of response it is while acting it out, the cadets do not get a point for the round.

KIRK SUGGESTS:

"Parents, feel free to use the following questions as a resource while you shepherd your child through situations of pride. It's often hard to discern what's going on in our hearts when we encounter challenging situations, so here are 4 questions that you can ask yourself and your children to help understand your motivation."

1. What happened that made you prideful?
2. What were you thinking or feeling?
3. What did you do in response?
4. How did your words and actions affect others?

These 4 questions are a helpful tool that were adapted from Paul David Tripp's book, *Age of Opportunity*."

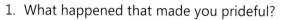

GAME #2 - PRESSED FOR TIME

LESSON

When we are humble, we think of others above ourselves.

OBJECTIVE

Valor is still struggling to be humble rather than prideful. BRAVE Cadets, help Valor and Kevin finish the race while showing humility to each other.

INSTRUCTIONS

1. The cadets will have 5 minutes to complete 10 tasks. The tasks must be completed one at a time.
2. The cadets will choose 1 person from their team to complete each task. The cadets will choose who does what task during the game, so make sure that the cadets don't plan ahead.
3. To start, the parent will read the first task aloud to the cadets. Each time they finish a task, the parent will read out the next task.

LIST OF TASKS

- Do 10 jumping jacks.
- Sing happy birthday 2 times.
- Touch all the pillows in the living room.
- High five one of your parents.
- Count how many doors are in the room.
- Name everyone in your family by their first name.
- Find 5 stuffed animals from around the house.
- Do 10 push ups.
- Find 5 pairs of socks from around the house.
- Say hello to everyone in your house by shaking their hand.

BRAVE TIP

Before playing the game, review how scoring works.

SCORING

- The cadets receive 1 point for every task they complete.
- The cadets lose 1 point for every time they took over another cadet's task.
- The cadets lose 1 point for every time they showed pridefulness during the game.
- The cadets receive 2 points if they displayed humility during the game (were encouraging or letting others go first).

TIME

Set a 5 minute timer before starting task #1.

TALK ABOUT IT

ONE CHILD MODIFICATION

Have the parent play with the cadet but have the cadet lead the decision making.

1. How would you define humility?

KIRK SUGGESTS:

"Humility is an attitude where you put others before yourself. For example, being thankful, being a good listener, encouraging others and seeing their gifts or skills, or even admitting when you are wrong."

2. In the game, you had to complete 10 tasks. Did you see anyone display humility as you played? If you saw pride, what was it that you did that demonstrated pride? What could you have done to have a more humble attitude?

3. In the story, Valor thought he was the perfect teammate for the raft race. Did Valor like it when Kevin joined his team? Why or why not?

4. Think of a time when you were being prideful. Why do you think you were prideful? How could you have responded differently if you were being humble?

5. When have you shown humility? Is it hard to be humble? Why or why not?

"Humble yourselves, therefore, under the mighty hand of God so that at the proper time he may exalt you, casting all your anxieties on him, because he cares for you."

1 Peter 5:6-7 (ESV)

TALLY UP THE POINTS TO SEE IF YOU WON!

FINAL THOUGHTS FROM KIRK

This book deals with something that all humans struggle with—pride (Proverbs 16:18 ESV). The selfish attitude of pride is at the root of our rebellion against God and causes us to sin against him (James 1:15 ESV). As much as we try to be humble and kind, we cannot, unless God himself helps us see our sin of pride and turn from it (2 Timothy 2:25 ESV). Thankfully, when we confess our sins and believe the Gospel of Jesus Christ, God transforms us on the inside, giving us a new heart with new desires that please him (2 Corinthians 5:17 ESV).